THE GOLDEN RULE OF SEX

The Poetry of Lovemaking

CHARLES MWEWA

DEDICATION

To us all – because love and sex made us!

CONTENTS

This book introduces the Golden Rule of Sex. The rule may be stated as: Do to or for your partner in sex what you would like them to do to or for you. This rule is exemplified, thus: Your sex must benefit your partner; your partner must participate to benefit you; and your own satisfaction is dependent upon your partner's satisfaction.

The book then debunks seven sex myths, thus: Size does not matter in sex, what matters is understanding; sex doesn't have to be made many times, what matters is the quality of the sexual act; there are no experts in sex (not even prostitutes), there are only willing participants; orgasm is not a chance stance, it can always be reached with mastery; there is no training required in sex (knowledge of *Kamasutra* is not necessary, either), all it takes is commitment; groaning doesn't happen to everyone during sex, some people can enjoy the entire episode without making a single sound; and there are no persons who are better at making love than others, there are only patient and impatient lovers.

And finally, the rule ends with the three principled quadrants of sexual happiness. These three quadrants are attitudinal; gratitudinal; and original. There are three attitudinal principles: Shared blanket; harlem consort; and cold-heat attitudes. There are three gratitudinal principles: Gratitude; fortitude, and altitude. And finally, there are three original principles. These are laugh-smile; give-receive; and security-safety.

c.m.

1 | GOLDEN RULE OF SEX

The Rule

Do to or for your partner in sex what you would like them to do to or for you.

Neural, Sensory and Motor Pleasure

Generally, sensorimotor processes involve the process of receiving sensory messages, also known as sensory input, to produce a response, known as motor output. Sensory information comes from our bodies and the environment around us through our sensory system. The sensory system may include vision, hearing, smell, taste, and touch. It may also include vestibular and proprioception processes.

Sexual behavior involves sensorimotor processes. But it is more; it is also regulated by both subcortical and cortical structures. Subcortical structures include the spinal cord, the hypothalamus and the brainstem. Cortical structures include occipital lobe, primary somatosensory cortex, parietal lobe, basal ganglia, frontal lobe, thalamus, cerebellum, etc. These cortical and subcortical structures act in concert to orchestrate an experience described as "primitive, complex, and versatile behavior."[1]

Sex's primitivity and versatility are understood. However, its complexity still remains a conundrum. This is because various processes and systems interact to produce a response which we call orgasm. These processes are dopaminergic (involves dopamine), serotonergic, cholinergic, adrenaline-related, and acetylcholine-stimulated transmitters. These, together with neuropeptides-intimated secretory routes, produce amazing sexual responses. In a layman's language, sexual activities are complex multi-collaborative responses through many neural and sensorimotor interactions. And these involve, literally, the entire neural and sensory systems. Sex

---

[1] "Neuroanatomy and function of human sexual behavior: A neglected or unknown issue?" https://www.ncbi.nlm.nih.gov/pmc/articles/PMC6908863 / assessed on December 1st, 2023.

is all-encompassing, bodily, souly, and spiritually.

Sex is quintessentially a sensual sensory pleasure. It involves all the five senses: Seeing, hearing, smelling, feeling and tasting. Sex is fundamentally all brainy, neural and very little hearty. However, sex can be an instrument of love – which is a matter of choice and not feeling (or sensory energy).

Sex has five sensory characteristics: Good to see; moody of what is heard; soother of bodily thrills; food for thought; and hoody of sensory smells. The five characteristics may be termed the Eve's Apple (no-one knows if the fruit Eve ate was an apple), from the Adamic fall mantra derived from Genesis 3:6-7:

> When the woman saw that the fruit
> of the tree was good for food and
> pleasing to the eye, and also
> desirable for gaining wisdom, she
> took some and ate it. She also gave
> some to her husband, who was with
> her, and he ate it. Then the eyes of
> both of them were opened, and they

realized they were naked; so, they
sewed fig leaves together and made
coverings for themselves.

There are false and true assumptions
made from this passage. Beginning with
the false assumptions. It is assumed
falsely that sex was the first sin that
entered the earth. And it is also a false
assumption that the fruit referenced in
this passage is an apple.

However, it could be true that the first
sin that entered into the world was rooted
in sensory perception. Thus, the woman
saw, heard, tasted, and by correct
assumptions, she smelt and felt. The
feeling is captured by the statement,
"…they realized they were naked; so, they
sewed fig leaves together and made
coverings for themselves."

Indeed, there is a reality to these
assumptions. But the practical truth is
that sex is among the most effective
pursuits that are clearly sensorimotor in
nature and scope.

Below, we briefly discuss each of the five sensory characteristics:

Good for Sight

Eyes are the windows of the brain, even of the soul. The sense of sight (seeing) sends and responds to the sexual stimuli. It awakens the brain to sensual awareness. Thus, it makes us want to do sex. Seeing begins the flow of the sensory universe which is a pleasure-anticipating receptor. In normal physiology, this is a chemical signal where a protein-ligand binds a protein receptor. The ligand is a chemical messenger released by one cell to signal either itself or a different cell.[2]

So, when we *see* human genitalia, we are moved to, or do, in fact, desire sex. The genitalia, too, is the focal point of the human eye's concentration. The first thing human eyes desire to see is the

[2] Eric J. Miller and Sarah L. Lappin, "Physiology, Cellular Receptor," StatPearls, September 14th, 2022.

genital configuration of the opposite sex's (or same sex's) important sexual areas, i.e., genitals, breasts and chests, hips, lips, etc., and many times, this is done unconsciously.

Mood Setter – what is heard

The sex pleasing sense is stimulated by the power of the ear. Women and men (women maybe more than men) delight in what they hear about themselves and the men. Reputation is a sexual stimulus, and the more women hear about a man the easier they can likely be attracted sexually.

The so-called love-language is, in fact, sexual talk. It is a brain-teaser that prompts people to be more assertive and even be better positioned for sex. What is said must be poetic (poetry of sex), stimulating and gracefully enchanting to captivating the hearing attention and sense.

The poetic language of sex must be descriptive and not prescriptive; sensual and not artificial. It must highlight those descriptive facets of the object of desire that are likely to endear and please them. The language that stimulates sexual senses must be commended with beautiful overtones and pleasing repertoires. To stimulate sex, what is heard must be romantic in nature, erotic in tune, and sexual in spirit. Men, for example, must reduce themselves to the level of a beggar who desires their wish, to the place where they are desperate hunters in search of a frill. That language easily awakens the woman's facilities to be had, possessed and to be hunted and caught.

On the contrary, bad, tasteless, demeaning and critical language puts men and women off sexually. No matter how attractive a man or woman is, if what the partners hears from them is incorrigible, it will hurt sex. Sex is the art of nice speech and the science of consistent praise.

Therefore, the sensual, sexual poet must create in the hearer a sense of being "known" that desires to hear more, leading to want to possess or be possessed. Indeed, saying nice things about your partner or spouse, and being heard, is a sexual stimulator, an aphrodisiac.

Rood of Senses – feel the bodily thrills

Men and women's genitalia are not the goal but the instrument. The goal is the holistic sensual pleasure. Sex is the only exercise that sets the sensual hooves loose. They are free to galivant. That is why there is an assumption of secrecy, confidentiality and place. The implication is that so lovers can be free to explore the universe called sex one with another.

Food for Thought

The sense of taste is a sound of pleasure. It can be the means to an end, or an end in itself. What may be termed as kissing, is very much a sex arousal activity that may lead or not lead to sex. Kissing involves an exchange of fluids through the mouth in a deliberate and wilful act. Kissing is a pleasurable activity. It may be done as an end in itself, or it may be a prerequisite to sexual intercourse.

A caveat is in order here, that unless verified in some form, oral kissing may be a health risk. The mouth can be a hoard of bacteria and even viruses. It is recommended to kiss only the partner you know you are familiar with their oral health hygiene and routines. Kissing carelessly or kissing people you do not know that very well may lead to unwanted infections and diseases.

The genitalia-mouth-interaction is very much an oral sexual interaction. In an oral sexual intercourse, pleasure is accomplished through the mouth orifice and but the exchange of saliva through the tongue is not necessarily oral sex.

Lips play an arousal role in oral, and even vaginal penetration, sex. The vaginal labia (euphemistically called "lips") play a similar role as in sexual arousal. "The labia minora (inner lips) are inside your outer lips. They begin at your clitoris and end under the opening to your vagina. Labia can be short or long, wrinkled or smooth. Often one lip is longer than the other. They also vary in color from pink to brownish black."[3]

The female clitoris and male glans are the center of pleasure (the feeling good sensation) and that is their main role in sexual intercourse. "[The] clitoris is made of spongy tissue that becomes swollen when you're aroused (turned on). It has thousands of nerve endings — more than any other part of the human body. And it's only purpose? To make you feel

---

[3] Planned Parenthood, "What are the parts of the female sexual anatomy?"
https://www.plannedparenthood.org/learn/health-and-wellness/sexual-and-reproductive-anatomy/what-are-parts-female-sexual-anatomy#:~:text=The%20labia%20minora%20(inner%20lips,from%20pink%20to%20brownish%20black. (accessed on December 3, 2023)

good."[4] Indeed, the same can be said about the glans.

Therefore, the combination of lips, the mouth and its contents (the tongue and saliva) and the clitoris or glans and the consummation thereof, constitute sexual tasting sensual pleasure. Participants in sexual arousal using the mouth are deliberate and they do desire to achieve the same arousal and pleasure they may derive from vaginal penetrating sex.

The mouth and its contents alone are not oral sex. Oral sex or oral copulation is the act of sexual contact between one person's mouth and another person's genitals or anus. It is perfectly legal when two adults who consent do it privately. There are two versions of oral copulation: *Cunnilingus* and *fellatio*. The former is oral sex performed on the vulva, while the latter is oral sex performed on the penis.

---

[4] *Ibid.*

Hood of Sensory Smell

The semen from penis and the vaginal discharges do have a familiar smell. We may call this the, "Sex Smell." This is different from the unhealthy odors women may discharge from time to time. Thus, "…the vagina has a familiar scent, which many do enjoy. Depending on the time of the month, vaginal discharge can change in smell (as well as consistency)."[5]

The smell of sex is an inviting atmosphere that many partners enjoy. However, one can only differentiate it from other smells when they have one constant partner. Having sex with multiple partners and frequent sex, may be dangerous – because it may maim the sex smell where one cannot distinguish unhealthy smells from the healthy ones.

An enjoyable smell from both men

---

[5] Claire Gillespie, "What Does a Healthy Vagina Smell Like? All vaginas have a scent—and no, it's not a bouquet of roses," Health.com, October 23, 2023

and women's genitalia and armpits may trigger sexual arousal in some men and women. All these are designed to heighten the sexual experience.

2 | SEX RULE EXEMPLIFICATION

Three Tenets

The golden rule of sex can be exemplified in three tenets. These tenets are: Your sex must benefit your partner; your partner must participate to benefit you; and your own satisfaction is dependent upon your partner's satisfaction.

Benefit Your Partner

True and satisfactory sex is aimed at benefiting the other partner, not yourself. The thinking that, "I must feel good," is a wrong attitude to take into a sex act. People respond differently to sex. Basically, there are two types of responses, especially in women. Some women are slow-burners, others are quick-fixers.

Slow-burner Types

Slow burners are usually compared to charcoal stoves. These are slow but on average, they produce a well simmered meal. To those who are impatient, slow burning can be very frustrating. But to those who desire a good and well-baked product, slow burners are ideal. There are no winners and losers. All it requires is to understand the sex type that you are dealing with.

Quick-fixer Types

These are men and women (usually, women) who have a very short sexual fuse. A small touch could light up the fire. They are overtly sexual sensitive. They respond to touches even in unassuming bodily areas where the charcoal-type would not be affected. Quick-fixer types meet their match in impatient men and women who can "reach' rather too quickly. With this type, a sexual encounter can be so brief that before you open your eyes, it is over.

Understanding is Key

Interestingly, and even, ironically, there is no better type; both types enjoy sex just the same. The only thing which differentiates the two types is time. To the slow-burner type, time is not of the essence. They are prepared to "enjoy" sex to the tilted end. This is not the case for the quick-fixer type. To them, time is not a factor at all. It can be over as soon as it begins.

Challenges begin to emerge where two partners of different sexual-typical pedigrees meet. Without understanding one another, frustration and nothing but frustration will be the order. At least one partner should be able to recognize the other's type on the spot and adjust.

Otherwise, their sexual encounter will be a disaster. The inability to understand these types puts off some people, even permanently. They might, mentally, be associating a sexual encounter with a drudge affair. They might even hate sex altogether. But when they meet a knowledgeable, understanding partner, it might rekindle their sexuality and catapult them to azure heights in sexual intercoursing.

Thus, in sex, understanding of the other partner's type is key; performance must of necessity be to benefit the other.

Participate to Benefit Them

Like the previous one, this exemplifies an attitude of "other focus." Sex is for your partner. They are the focal point. This means that you will be considerate. Consider time, place, and prevailing circumstances.

If it depended upon that, would the sexual encounters have happened? This is an important question to ask yourself. Sometimes, partners may give verbal signals, and some other times, non-verbal. If your partner says that they are tired, they may be signaling that they are not ready for sex that day or at that time.

Traditionally, men, especially, have been taught, erroneously, that sex must be had anytime, everywhere and anywhere. That is a wrong teaching. Women, whether single or married, have many challenges to contend with before they can get in the "mood" for uninterrupted sex. They may even be undergoing their monthly regimes (menstruation). Or they may be concerned with bills, children, if any, or other more pressing concerns. A man must understand. Men and women do not die from sexual starvation. A brief moment to deal with emergencies or pressing concerns will not maim the marriage or relationship, either.

The responsibility to please the partner applies to women pleasing men as well. Some men may be impatient and want to ejaculate (early-comers as it were). Others may take long. Generally, slower-comer men are capable of satisfying any woman type, *ceteris paribus*. However, this is not a ground rule, it may be an exception to the rule, at best. What it cogent, nevertheless, is understanding and asking relevant questions.

Although sex is a neural-sensory-mental-motor activity, it can easily be controlled. Asking the right questions before, during and even in the "cooling period," of a sexual interaction, may save a relationship from failing, sexually.

Partners, interestingly, may be more willing to advise on how they might want the sexual encounter to be performed, so, adhere to that. The assumption that once naked the sexual encounter must happen is a fallacy. It is also not correct that penetration, for example, must happen when you feel like.

Partners must be sensitive to each other's sensual needs throughout their partnership. Some people have wrong ideas that they would be punishing their spouses by "starving" them of sex. That is a myth – humans cannot be starved of sex; they simply change their preferences. Starving a partner of sex is the quickest way to destroying a good relationship.

Be Satisfied Only When They Are

This is the final exemplification of the sex rule. Your own satisfaction comes last in sex. First things first, and your partner is first, when it comes to sex. They are first in mind, soul and body. So, more than just being considerate, be patient, ask questions, if possible, and study your partner's reactions and temperature and temperamental fluctuations. Everything is on the table – the manner in which they talk, make noise or not, breathe or groan, their physical or positional preferences, etc., all these may be a clue as to their mentality and temperament during the sexual encounter.

The duty of the partner is to please the partner in sex *by all means possible*, as long as it is legal, ethical and respectable. If the peni or virginal penetration cannot do it, invent some other tactics till the partner has "reached." Their happiness in sex is your happiness, too.

3 | SEVEN SEX MYTHS

Seven Myths

The seven sex myths to be busted are: Size does not matter in sex, what matters is understanding; sex doesn't have to be made many times, what matters is the quality of the sexual act; there are no experts in sex (not even prostitutes), there are only willing participants; orgasm is not a chance stance, it can always be reached with mastery; there is no training required in sex (knowledge of *Kamasutra* is not necessary, either), all it takes is commitment; groaning doesn't happen to everyone during sex, some people can enjoy the entire episode without making a single sound; and there are no persons who are better at making love than others, there are only patient and impatient lovers.

Size Does Not Matter in Sex

When it comes to sex, size does not matter. But understanding matters. The nudity industry tries to burden society with the illusion of an over-sized penis and a tighter vagina as ideals in sex imaginations. Indeed, to some women who are used to meeting several men for sex, size may be an issue owing to those women's vaginal expansiveness. But even in those instances, the woman's anatomy is adept at readjusting itself, especially when given a breathing space.

Some men with extremely very large peni could be a danger to their women. Extremely large peni could cause browsing to the birth canal or even mentally to the psychology of sex itself. It could also make penetration extremely painful. In many of those situations, women have to use lubricants just to ease off the pain of penetration.

Extremely small peni are not a disadvantage, either. The vagina's most sensitive part, the clitoris and the surrounding membranes, only need enough contact to be stimulated. The thrusting of the penis with vigorous spurts (euphemistically referred to as screwing) showcased by moving cinemas and the pornographic industry are an exaggeration of the reality.

Men's instruments can handle any female genitalia, no matter the size. And women's instruments can handle any man, no matter the size. What is required is understanding. Knowing how one relates to their man or woman's genitalia is a deliberate undertaking. This is necessary because the aim is to please, and not to be pleased. With understanding, every sexual encounter could be a moment of bliss and not endurance.

Frequency of Sex is Not a Big Issue

Sex does not have to be made many times; what matters is the quality of the sexual act. Quality, and not quantity, is important to sex. Those who teach that sex must be made many times over are mistaken. Reality does not allow for that unless sex is one's trade or profession. Even those who are in the sex industry do understand this requirement. They must often relax and rest their instruments to perform excellently.

Sex must be a sacred endeavor only undertaken when there is need. There are various sexual needs. Some of these could be for procreation, for sustaining a healthy relationship, for relaxing, for romantic occasions, for catharsis, for protest, etc. Each of these moments must be purposeful and respectful. Even human sexual genitalia needs rest to recharge. Men need a dull moment to allow for semen reproduction; and women need time to deal with their menstrual contingencies. In either case, a healthy relationship needs some sexual activities, but not all the time.

It is not the intention of the author to prescribe how many times sex must be made in a relationship. Each partnership must access the practicality of some sex without sacrificing the sanity of the parties or giving effect to infidelity. Too little sex in a relationship may be injurious to the healthy and comfort of the partners. Too much sex may be unhealthy or even nerve-racking.

There are No Experts in Sex

Not even prostitutes are experts at sex. Generally, every home entertains some sort of sexual activity. Sex is like driving. Everyone with a valid driver's license can drive – some better than others – but all can drive.

Some people think that they need or must practice sex to be perfect. That is not necessary, either. Sex is the only human endeavor that does not need or does not warrant practice. Every sexual encounter is unique and cannot be replicated. With sex, practice, in fact, makes worse, unless it is practice with the same consistent partner. Sex with many sexual partners does not improve sexual performance. It hurts conscience.

Because of the uniqueness of sex, the more partners one entertains, the more stressful, disappointing, and disoriented they get. Sex with one partner is the healthiest and most secure form of enjoying the endeavor. Because with sex, many things are involved (mind, soul, body, spirit and trust), a partner can only achieve ascendancy with a partner they know, love, and understand. In other words, to enjoy sex, trust must be present. Without trust, both men and women may simply be going through movements, as it were, mere fleshly playing, but devoid of the spirit of pleasure itself.

Orgasm is Not a Chance Stance

Sex is designed to be orgasmic. Orgasm is the height of the sexual arousal. It is also known as sexual climax. It is sudden. It is rhythmic. It is exciting. As muscles in the pelvic region contract, they release convulsions of highly discharged and accumulated sexual excitement. The enormity of these spontaneous rhythmic contractions releases this unspeakable sexual pleasure we call orgasm.

It is a win-lose situation, for both men and women. If it becomes a win-win situation, there is deficiency and partners may not be said to consummate their sexual encounters.

Rule of thumb, each partner must do all they can to make the other partner reach orgasm. If possible, the partner who gets there first must wait for the other partner to arrive. That is the goal of a sexual encounter. Anything less than that is a joke and may not be different from a rape encounter. Orgasm is mastery; it is not chance.

Sex is best when the participants are willing to do it. Any moment of force, coercion or tricking may be abusiveness. This does not matter whether couples are married, partners have been together long, or with a sex service worker. Sex must respect the essence of human dignity whether it is paid for or it is free.

Training is Unnecessary to Sex

There is no training required in sex (knowledge of the famous *Kamasutra* is not necessary, either). Animals do sex without training; they simply know. Insects do sex without training; they simply know. And so are humans. No-one should be worried that they do not know how to perform sex or that they have never done it before.

In fact, first timers are better equipped to reaching an orgasm than regulars. Sex is an innate functionality; it can be improved upon only with understanding. But that is always a unified objective between two partners. Sex education only provides the fundamentals. It does not institute the culture. The so-called sex gurus are not gurus at all; they all encounter sex differentially; no two encounters are the same. Sex is a speech of nature, and everyone whose moment has arrived, will be able to speak it, fluently.

Noise during Sex is a Myth

With sex, all it takes is commitment; groaning doesn't happen to everyone during sex. Some people can enjoy the entire episode without making a single sound. The sexual posturing reminiscent of Hollywood movies (and now being mimicked by Bollywood, Nollywood, etc.) are myths.

Indeed, a sexual encounter can be as enjoyable but as cold as winter at the same time. Or it can still be enjoyable and trending at the apex of the summer season. Individual idiosyncrasies loom large when it comes to how men and women react to orgasmic spurts.

Some shout, others are quiet. Some cry, others laugh. Some bite, others kiss. Some close their eyes, others open them. Some say many things (even unintelligible blubbing), others are as quiet as a cemetery. Some call names, others endear their loved ones. In short, there is no single way of responding to orgasms. Each person must appreciate the way their partner reacts and must live with that.

No-one is Better at Love-making

There is nothing like one ounce of love which is better than the other. Love is love. When it comes to love-making, no-one does it better than another. There is, though, something like a more patient, more understanding, and more sensitive partner than the other.

There are no persons who are better at making love than others, there are only patient and impatient lovers. Anyone can make good love. Anyone can give good sex. Anyone can satisfy their partner. All it takes is a goal to make the other happier in sex than oneself.

The rule must stand, do all and everything to satisfy your partner as you would like your parent to satisfy you in sex. That is what is meant by *love*-making.

4 | PRINCIPLES OF SEXUAL HAPPINESS

Three Quadrants

The sex principles can be divided into three quadrants: Attitudinal; gratitudinal; and original. There are three attitudinal principles: Shared blanket; harlem consort; and cold-heat attitude. There are three gratitudinal principles: Gratitude; fortitude, and altitude. Finally, there are three original principles: Laugh-smile; give-receive; and security-safety.

Attitudinal Principles

Shared Blanket

Sex is like a shared blanket attitude. Everyone must be tucked comfortably inside. When one turns, the other must be taken into consideration. One blanket must comfort both participants equally.

Harlem Consort

In olden days, the queen was the figurehead of the Harlem, facilitating the sexual intercourse between her husband, the king, and the other members of the Harlem. The consort was loved and endeared by the king, but she always had to have the best interest of other concubines. Sex is the same. Participants are there to be valued and enjoyed but only if they must satisfy the *king* and her *queen*.

Cold-Heat

Everyone knows that extreme heat or extreme cold are undesirable but the middle is necessary. In a relationship, partners must equalize their own feelings with those of their partners. The goal is balance. And that is the true meaning of being kept warm by one's partner, the warmth of a partnership.

Gratitudinal Principles

Gratitude

Sex must be performed from the gratitude point of view, not struggle or force. Participants should be able to thank their partners at the end of the encounter.

Fortitude

Sex, by definition, ensures the exerting of strength. Sometimes, men and women must endure the encounter until it is thoroughly performed. So, couples and partners must be prepared mentally and physically to participate in the encounter.

Sex is work and partners must do their best to hold and be held, give and receive and endure despite the discomfort that they might experience. Love is the key to endurance. Because partners love each other, they must be willing to give of themselves even when they might experience some painful discomfiture.

Altitude

Indeed, sex is like climbing a mountain until one reaches the peak. When climbing, there is energy exerted and fatigue could be the norm. But climbers understand that they must keep on going until they reach the summit. Those who are not willing to reach the summit must not embark on this natural process called sex. Some people think that everything will be roses in the sexual encounter, that is a fallacy. Roses have thorns, so does sex. Love trumps huddles. And those who will satisfy their partners are ready for any eventuality. All becomes settled after reaching the orgasmic summit.

Original Principles

Laugh-smile

What sets sex apart is the relief that comes at the end. It can be summarized into laughing or smiling. So, all the efforts and the endurance paid can be accounted for – because at the end, the partners should feel like laughing or smiling.

Give-receive

Sex involves giving and receiving. It is a mutual intercourse. When a successful sexual encounter has been experienced, partners feel like they are useful because they have been able to give something good and valuable. In turn, they also feel like they have received something good and of value.

Security-safety

The relief that comes after a good sexual encounter reassures security and safety. The partners feel that they have invested in profitable ventures, that their partners will go an extra mile to protect that which is meaningful to them and to each other. Sex must culminate into feelings of safety and security.

ABOUT THE AUTHOR

Award-Winning, Best-Selling Author, Charles Mwewa (LLB; BA Law; BA Ed; LLM), is a prolific researcher, poet, novelist, lawyer, law professor and Christian apologist and intercessor. Mwewa has written no less than 100 books and counting in every genre and has exhibited his works at prestigious expos like the Ottawa International Book Expo and is the winner of the Coppa Awards for his signature publication, *Zambia: Struggles of My People.*
Mwewa and his family live in the Canadian Capital City of Ottawa.

SELECTED BOOKS BY THIS AUTHOR

1. *ZAMBIA: Struggles of My People (First and Second Editions)*
2. *10 FINANCIAL & WEALTH ATTITUDES TO AVOID*
3. *10 STRATEGIES TO DEFEAT STRESS AND DEPRESSION: Creating an Internal Safeguard against Stress and Depression*
4. *100+ REASONS TO READ BOOKS*
5. *A CASE FOR AFRICA?S LIBERTY: The Synergistic Transformation of Africa and the West into First-World Partnerships*
6. *DECOLONIZATION: Reclaiming African Originality and Destiny*
7. *A PANDEMIC POETRY, COVID-19*
8. *ALLERGIC TO CORRUPTION: The Legacy of President Michael Sata of Zambia*
9. *BOOK ABOUT SOMETHING: On Ultimate Purpose*
10. *CAMPAIGN FOR AFRICA: A Provocative Crusade for the Economic and Humanitarian Decolonization of Africa*
11. *CHAMPIONS: Application of Common Sense and Biblical Motifs to Succeed in Both*

103.   ONTARIO PARALEGAL LICENSING EXAMINATION:
Civil Litigation, Questions & Answers
104.   WINNING RESOLUTIONS: A Treatise

INDEX

soul, 21, 29
spinal cord. *See* subcortical
spirit, 8, 29
spontaneous rhythmic contractions. *See* orgasm
starving, 21
strength, 38
Struggles of My People, 41, 43
subcortical, 2
sudden. *See* orgasm
summer, 32

T

tenets, 15
thalamus. *See* cortical
The Rule, 1
the West, 43
time, 19
tongue, 10, 12
tricking. *See* wllling
trust, 29
two types of responses, 16

U

understanding, ix, 18, 20, 23, 24, 26, 31, 33
unspeakable sexual pleasure. *See* orgasm

V

vagina, 11, 13, 25
vaginal penetration, 10
value, 40
verbal signals, 19
versatile behavior, 3
viruses, 10
vulva, 12

W

warmth of a partnership, 37
willing, 30
winter, 32

Z

Zambia, 41, 43, 44, 45, 46